**For my husband, Booth, who shares my passion for old houses,
and for my father, Bob, who wanted to be an architect
once upon a time. — N. L.**

**A special thanks to some friends who helped me work the bugs out:
Victoria Rock and the Chronicle Kids Department, Chauni Haslet, Kim and
Carol in Fremont, Dr. John Beasley, Bill Burbank, and Sarah Boykin.**

Book design by Catherine Jacobes.
Typeset in Syntax and AdLib.
The art in this book was done in mixed-media collage, created with different kinds of paper,
parts of images cut from old catalogs and magazines, wood veneers, cork veneer,
blueprints, cardboard, skeleton leaves, old engravings, stickers, etc., that were glued onto
Arches Hot Press Watercolor paper and painted with Holbein Acryla Gouache.
It was all done by hand. No computers were used.
Manufactured in China.

Library of Congress Cataloging-in-Publication Data
Laden, Nina.
Roberto : the insect architect / by Nina Laden.
p.   cm.
Summary: Roberto the architect, who also happens to be a
termite, sets off to the city to find success.
ISBN 0-8118-2465-9
[1. Termites—Fiction.] I. Title.
PZ7.L13735 Ro   2000
[E]—dc21   99-050851   CIP

Distributed in Canada by Raincoast Books
9050 Shaughnessy Street, Vancouver, British Columbia V6P 6E5
10 9 8 7 6 5 4

Chronicle Books LLC
85 Second Street, San Francisco, California 94105

www.chroniclekids.com

ROBERTO
The Insect Architect

Nina Laden

chronicle books · san francisco

Even when Roberto was little, **he went against the grain.** Like most termites, he melted over maple, and pined for pine. Oak was okay, too. But Roberto didn't eat his food. He played with it.

"You're wasting a good meal," his mother said. "Don't you know there are termites starving in Antarctica?" But Roberto didn't answer. He was busy daydreaming about becoming a famous architect.

Insect Inquirer
ROBERTO BUILDS FIRST HOUSE ON MOON

WOOD CHIPS

"Whoever heard of a termite who wanted to be an architect?" the other termites snickered. "Roberto, you should be a chef!" But Roberto didn't want to cook. He wanted to build. **Hungry to start a new life,** Roberto realized he had to leave.

So Roberto packed his bags and took the train to Bug Central Station, in the busy, buzzing hive of the big city. The city was a place where you could **build your dreams.** It was a place where you would be accepted. It was a place where the other termites wouldn't bug you. Roberto beamed hope like a lit-up skyscraper.

But **hope didn't come cheap** in the big city. Neither did a place to live. Roberto had no choice but to rent a room in a flea-bag hotel run by a nervous tick. He shared the room with a family of bed bugs. Roberto introduced himself. Then he built the bed bugs their very own beds.

After a good night's sleep, Roberto began to look for work as an architect. But things didn't go very well.

"Show me what you've done,"
said the architect,
Hank Floyd Mite.

"There are no termites in my houses,"
stated Fleas Van Der Rohe.

"I'm busy," Antonia Gaudi blurted out.

"Don't BUG me!"

As Roberto crawled home, **feeling like a pest,** he was sideswiped by a fly. "Watch where you're going," he mumbled. The fly started to cry.

"But I don't have any place to go," she lamented.

Roberto wanted to comfort her, but he was nearly nailed by a carpenter ant trying to fix a rickety shed. Then out of nowhere, Roberto was almost run over by a stampede of roaches being chased from a diner. And suddenly, a frantic ladybug flew into his arms.

"My house is on fire and my children are gone!" the ladybug cried.

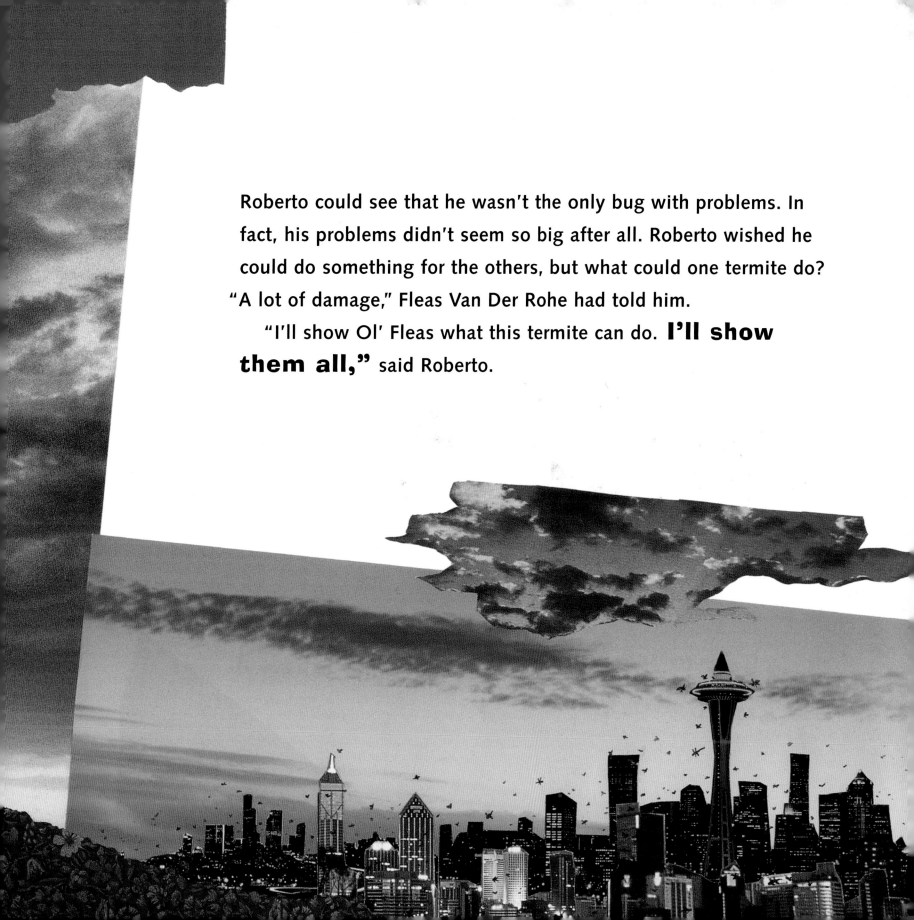

Roberto could see that he wasn't the only bug with problems. In fact, his problems didn't seem so big after all. Roberto wished he could do something for the others, but what could one termite do? "A lot of damage," Fleas Van Der Rohe had told him.

"I'll show Ol' Fleas what this termite can do. **I'll show them all,**" said Roberto.

Back at the hotel, Roberto **came up with a plan.** First, he drew up some blueprints. He sketched houses and streets. He sketched stores and playgrounds. By the time he was finished, he had sketched an entire neighborhood. "Now I just need to find a good location," he declared.

Roberto searched all over the city for the perfect site. He finally found an abandoned, run-down block of crumbling buildings. It was a total mess. There were piles of old wood and garbage everywhere. **It was just what he was looking for.**

Roberto hammered and nailed.

He sawed and sanded.

He worked day and night.

Like a magician, he transformed the block of junk into a street of extraordinary homes. Each one was **a work of art.** But Roberto didn't sign his artwork. Instead he anonymously sent the keys to the new owners. Then he rolled up his plans and went home.

Some very surprised bugs went home, too. Tudor, the fly with no place to go, buzzed with delight.

"I am a house fly again," she declared.

Then Grant, the carpenter ant, arrived. He dropped his tool belt on the porch.

"Now I can have a real workshop," he beamed.

The roaches were the next ones on the scene.

"You won't find us sleeping in salads anymore," they rejoiced.

Finally, Dotty, the ladybug, and her children moved into their new lair.

"It's perfect," she sighed. "It's fireproof!"

Quickly, word spread. Soon everyone wanted to know
who built these amazing abodes. Rumors were flying.
Antennae were buzzing.

Barbara Waterbugs
wanted an exclusive interview.

Robin Leech promised to
make the builder rich and famous.

Steven Shieldbug wanted the movie rights.

Diane Spider searched the World Wide Web for the scoop.

And **The Insect Inquirer** offered a reward to the first bug who brought the builder to light.

All day long, bounty-hunting butterflies took wing.
Paper wasps swarmed the streets. Bold weevils
crawled out of the woodwork. But late at night,
a click beetle got the shot.

The next morning,
headlines screamed the news.

INSECT INQUIRER

"TERMITE CHIPS NEW HOMES OUT OF OLD BLOCKS!"

"It's Roberto," Tudor hummed.

He's our HERO!

Overnight, Roberto became **the talk of the town.** Architects offered him jobs. Book publishers wanted his story. Ladybugs sent him love letters. And his bug buddies threw him a big bash. At the height of the party, the Mayor unveiled a statue of Roberto to be placed in the city park.

ROBERTO
INSECT ARCHITECT

WINGFLY MUSEUM

Roberto built his dream. He opened his own company and became the most famous architect in the insect world. Students studied him in school. Some of his houses even became museums.

But best of all, when little termites play with their food, now their parents say:

"Be creative!"

Maybe someday you'll grow up to be just like Roberto."

INSECT INQUIRER

EXTRA!

ROBERTO BUILDS
FIRST HOUSE ON MARS